# Triple Gold Star!
★★★

# Tracy Beaker
## The Story of Me

**ALL NEW** Tracy Beaker story inside! →

You can only read it here!

I give it 10 out of 10!

Turn over for totally tremendous stuff!

# A-Z of Me!

I dare you to read this page about the Brave and Brilliant Tracy Beaker!

## Amazing

Actually, I'm the greatest kid in the whole world. In fact, my story is incredible, dynamic and heart-rending. Honest.

## Being in care

Living in The Dumping Ground is rubbish. I've had two foster families, but they didn't work out. I'm working on changing that very soon!

## Cam

My best friend and fellow-writer. I'm hoping she could be my new foster Mum.

← Cam

## Disneyland

I could go there with my real mum and eat loads of burgers and drink strawberry milkshakes and meet Mickey Mouse. My real mum's very glamorous...

Elaine ↓

## Elaine The Pain

That's my oh-so-boring social worker. We talk about all sorts of Tremendously Tedious things but never about my mum because that's

**Strictly private!**

## Fib

I tell a lot of these, according to Mike and Jenny. I'm just prone to exaggerating because I'm a writer, so I don't think I'm actually fibbing — just being creative!

## Greatest

I'm the greatest girl ever and it's obvious that I'm going to grow up to be a best-selling author. Cam says I'm a born writer so I'll probably be very rich and famous when I grow up...

## Hay Fever

I absolutely never cry, but sometimes I'm prone to really bad bouts of hay fever that make my eyes water quite a lot.

## In trouble

Sometimes I pretend to be a ghost and scare the little ones in The Dumping Ground. I'm definitely in serious trouble when I do that!

## If I was...

Older, I would...........................................................................................
............................................................................................

An awesome author, I would.............................................................
............................................................................................

A kitten, I would............................................................................
............................................................................................

Yelled at, I would...........................................................................
............................................................................................

Invisible, I would............................................................................
............................................................................................

Very tall, I would............................................................................
............................................................................................

Very rich, I would...........................................................................
............................................................................................
............................................................................................

Tracy's dream
house!

# Child Of The Week!

Create your very own Star Of The Week poster!

I made this terrific poster. Who wouldn't want to adopt this little angel?

## Tracy Beaker

Have you a place in your hearts for dear little Tracy? Brilliant and beautiful, this little girl needs a loving home. Very rich parents preferred, as little Tracy needs lots of toys, presents and pets to make up for her Totally Tragic past.

### Now make your own perfect poster:

☆ Write your name at the top — make the letters really bright!

☆ Write all the completely fabulous facts about yourself in the right hand section.

☆ Finish with a lovely drawing of you!

Elaine

# Tracy

Tracy is a lively, healthy, chatty, ten-year-old who has been in care for a number of years. Consequently she has a few behaviour problems and needs firm loving handling in a long-term foster home.

The real poster that Elaine–The–Pain made of me is rubbish!

## Now make your own real poster:

⭐ Write your name in the top section in block writing.
⭐ In the right hand box, tell people all about you — even the naughty bits!
⭐ Draw a picture of your face in the left hand box.

# Beaker Blushes!

## TEAR TRAUMA

You go to the cinema with your besties and see a really sad film. Then you bump into a whole group of boys from your school while you're sobbing like a baby with swollen eyes.

**You Say:**

Imagine you thinking that I'm crying! That's ridiculous! I don't ever cry — I'm just suffering from an incredibly bad bout of hay fever. Yes, it affects me at all times of year. If you shared your popcorn with me that would make me feel a whole lot better, hint, hint, hint...

## PANTS

You go to school accompanied by a pair of pants which have stuck to the back of your trousers in the tumble dryer. Mean girls are mocking you.

**You Say:**

Didn't you know it's a tip-top joke trend to wear pants on your trousers? Personally, I think I look beautiful. Better than all of you stupid creeps. I'm the greatest!

## SLEEP TALK

You stay over at a friend's house and wake everyone up by talking loudly in your sleep. Her brother tells all his friends who are giggling every time you walk past.

**You Say:**

Ha! If you knew anything you'd realise that only the most intelligent human beings talk in their sleep. Clearly I'm BRILLIANT and you lot are just STUPID...

## FALLING FOR YOU

You take a short-cut through the park and slide down a muddy slope, arriving at school late and covered in leaves and dirt. Your teacher is less than impressed.

**You Say:**

Actually, I'm all dirty because I stopped a robbery, quick as a wink, in the park earlier. Scotland Yard will probably be along to take my statement shortly. The Chief Constable said I was Simply Amazing and you'll probably see me on the news tonight...

Justine

BOG OFF!

No peeking!

THE Tracy FILES

KEEP OUT!

Strictly private!

For Tracy's eyes ONLY!

Elaine    Mike    Peter    Justine    Cam    Carly

# Name:
## Elaine The Pain

# Job:
## MY Social worker.

Well, actually, she's the social worker for all the kids in the Dumping Ground. Honestly, it's bad enough we have to share our toys and sweets — we even have to split a social worker in this dump. At least there's plenty of Elaine to go round, ha ha!

Yes, really.

# Qualifications:

I'm afraid Big–Wobbly–Bum–Elaine The Pain just doesn't have the Required Skills to manage us lot, especially a child as Emotionally Fragile and Tragically Institutionalised as the magnificent Tracy Beaker.

Champion Tracy

## CONFIDENTIAL INFORMATION

Elaine thinks she's so clever when she uses all these stupid social worker words to describe me. Well, I've got her sussed! Elaine says I'm special. Yeah, right. It doesn't take a genius to work out what she *really* means...

**Special** = A proper handful.

Oh, and I'm also:
**Lively** = Difficult.
**Chatty** = Cheeky.
**Creative** = Destructive.
**Needs a firm, loving hand** = Serious behavioural problems.

Avoid at all costs!

# Name: Mike

## Job:

Mike looks after us with Jenny.

Jenny

I suppose you could say he's our carer. He isn't half a bore, always banging on about Rules and Responsibility. Yawn!

# Qualifications:

I don't know, do I? He drives us to school in the minibus but apart from that he's pretty useless. I mean, how hard can it be to look after a bunch of Beautifully Behaved kids like us?

Mike's not a bad old stick actually. He did sneak me a plate of spag bol once (my all-time favourite) when I'd been sent to my room after an Unfortunate Incident involving my fist and Justine-Had-It-Coming-Littlewood's big nose.

## CONFIDENTIAL INFORMATION

Huh, Mike doesn't have any Deadly Embarrassing secrets. Boring. He never says bad words or loses his temper with us — he doesn't even pick his nose when he thinks no-one's looking. Ah-hah! I did see him sneak a slice of cake when Jenny's back was turned. The very last slice of Jenny's extra-chocolatey, marvellously gloopy chocolate cake, as it happens. I wonder if Mike will give me an extra-big box of Smarties in exchange for my Eternal Silence...

sweeties ↘

yum!

17

# Name:
## Peter Ingham

*Weedy!*

Otherwise known as Peetie-Weetie, Snivelling Creep, Wimpy Peter... I could go on and on and on.

# Job:
## ~~I'm Tracy's bestest friend.~~

As if, Peter-No-Mates! Tracy Beaker doesn't need friends, especially a drip like you. Bog off and play with the other little children, Peter Ingham!

# Qualifications:

If snivelling and whining was an Olympic event Peter would win gold every time. He trails behind me everywhere I go, dragging his little feet and simpering his silly smile. He reckons we're best mates just because we happen to share the same birthday. He's so wet and weedy.

## CONFIDENTIAL INFORMATION

This is TOP SECRET, right? I have a Very Small Problem at night-time. I stupidly told Louise about it, back when she was my best friend, and she only went and told Justine Needs-To-Mind-Her-Own-Business Littlewood. Anyway, I bumped into Peter in the middle of the night with his arms full of bed sheets and it turns out he's wet in more ways than one. I teased him a bit but then I felt bad and now we're sort of mates.

# Name:
Justine Number–One–Enemy Littlewood

It's a miracle she hasn't broken every mirror in the Dumping Ground with <u>that</u> hideous mug.

Justine

# Job:
Most Irritating Girl In The <u>Whole</u> Wide World.

# Qualifications:

She thinks she's so special at absolutely everything but she has Considerably NO Talent whatsoever. She can't draw for toffee and she has Severely Limited Imagination. You should take a look at her Life Story book — it's Positively Tedious and Mind–numbingly Boring.

## CONFIDENTIAL INFORMATION

Justine ratted on me when I accidentally broke her Mickey Mouse clock THROUGH NO FAULT OF MY OWN. Doesn't she know anything?! The first rule of the Dumping Ground is NEVER sneak on ANYONE. Just you wait, Justine Tell–Tale Littlewood. I'll get my revenge soon.

## DASTARDLY PAYBACK PLANS

PLAN A —
Ultimate Humiliation!

PLAN B —
Deliver a karate chop death blow!

Black belt Tracy

# Name:
## Camilla

It's so much more glamorous than plain old Cam. Though there's nothing at all glam about Cam. Hey, that rhymes!

## Job: Prospective Foster Mother to the Brave and Brilliant Tracy Beaker!

And she's a writer. Sort of. I keep nagging her to get her act together and write a whopping great bestseller so she can buy me lots of cool designer clothes and whisk me away to a tropical island in a private jet, natch.

## ~~Qualifications:~~
## Foster Parent Potential

~~Wealthy~~

~~Successful~~

~~Buys lots of presents~~

~~Fashionable~~ Are you kidding?!

Generous ✓ — Well, she does take me to McDonald's on Saturdays — yum yum!

Loving ✓

## CONFIDENTIAL INFORMATION

I'm going to move in with Cam! Just until my real mum comes to get me, of course. We'll live in a stylish city apartment with a huge balcony and lounge on pristine leather sofas, a big box of chocs in one hand and a strawberry milkshake in the other...

Who am I kidding? There isn't room to swing a cat in Cam's tiny flat! And it's a bit of a dump, what with her scruffy furniture. Cam's flat isn't exactly the latest in interior design, but at least it's *home*.

Cam

# Name:
## Carly Beaker

My mum's the best!

# Job:
## The Bestest, Most Prettiest Mum Ever!

My mum's such a great actress and so totally drop-dead gorgeous all the big Hollywood producers want her for their movies. That's why she's always too busy to come and see me.

## ~~Qualifications:~~
### Best Things About My Mum

1. She's so glamorous and beautiful. I wish I took after her.
2. When she's in a good mood she lets me dress up in her most fashionable clothes and we have a right laugh.
3. When I was a little kid Mum bought me a Very Expensive and Extremely Delicate china doll. I'm not really into dolls but I loved Bluebell because she always reminded me of Mum. She got spoiled when some rotten kid at the Dumping Ground poked out her big blue eyes with a biro. Typical.
4. She said she'll try to come and see me at Christmas. So ya boo sucks to you Justine Pea-brain Littlewood!

Carly + Tracy forever

## CONFIDENTIAL INFORMATION

The Dumping Ground

Mum swears she'll come and take me away from the Dumping Ground one day. Elaine The Pain says I shouldn't get my hopes up and that Mum shouldn't make promises she can't keep, but I just know we'll live happily ever after, just the two of us.

Carly

I ♥ Mum

# How To Draw Carly!

Draw your own Sharratt-style picture with our step-by-step guide!

**1.** Start by drawing a U shape with two little ears for Carly's face. Then add in her wild wavy hair! Draw Carly's neck and arms and the top of her dress. Don't forget her pearls!

**2.** Add in some detail! Finish Carly's dress, draw her hands and her drop earrings.

**3.** Draw the sofa and Carly's glamorous high heeled shoe. The sofa ends are like squished ear shapes! Sketch Carly's facial features. Draw a glitzy crystal chandelier for her too!

22

4. Add a pattern to Carly's dress, finish her earrings and draw in her other shoe. Add legs to the sofa plus a carpet. Give Carly a glossy, pouting mouth and long eyelashes. Now colour in your picture.

Nick's Tip!
Make the chandelier really sparkle by adding white lines around it!

Strictly private!

# Tracy's Sudoku Snacks

Can you fit Tracy and her fave snacks into the grid? Every row, column and mini-grid must contain one of each item.

Tracy

burger
yum!

milkshake
yum!

ice lolly
yum!

french fries
yum!

birthday cake
yum!

Solution:

24

# Tracy Beaker Party Time!

The greatest ever guide to brilliant birthdays and super-cool celebrations!

I ❤ presents!

Hint, hint, hint!

# Brilliantly Beastly Bat-vites!

Make party invites TB-style!

## You'll need:
- ★ Black paper cut into 16cm squares
- ★ Stick-on gems
- ★ White or silver pen

**1.** Fold a square of paper from corner to corner to make a triangle. Measure down 4cm from the long edge and draw a line.

**2.** Fold the top down toward the point along the line.

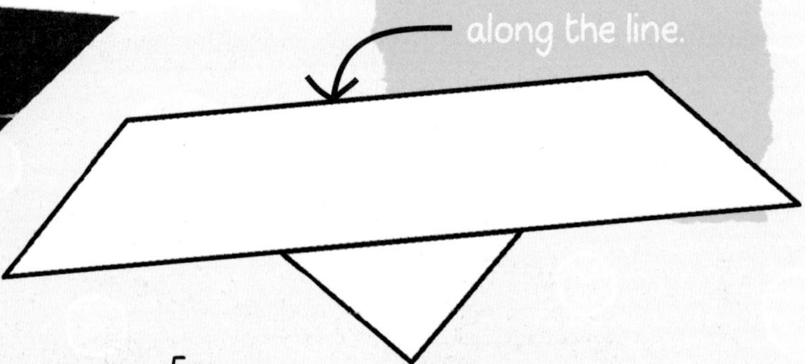

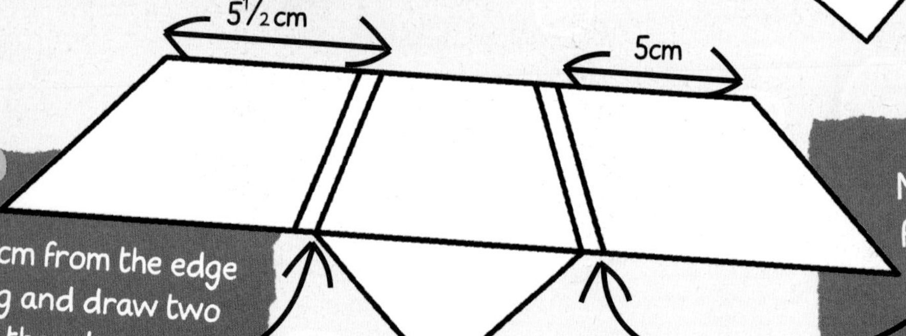

5½cm

5cm

**3.** Measure 5½cm from the edge of each wing and draw two lines to meet the edges of the point here.

Measure ½cm away from your first lines and draw another two like this.

27

**4.** Fold each end forward towards you along the first lines you drew. Crease and unfold.

**5.** Fold each end back along the second lines you drew. Crease and unfold. These folds will make the bat body stand out from the wings.

**6.** Turn over. Mark a notch for the ears and curves on the wings then carefully cut out the shapes

Come to my spooky party!

6 o'clock on Saturday October 31st

from Tracy

21 Greenside Street Dress up!

**7.** Flip over to the other side again and write your invite on the back of the bat.

**8.** Finish by sticking some glowing red gem eyes to the front and drawing on two spooky fangs.

Eeeek!

# Shocking Snacks!

*I dare you to eat these creepy-crawly snacks!*

## WORMS in DIRT

Remember when Tracy ate a worm in *The Dare Game*? Now you can do the same...

## YOU WILL NEED

- ☆ Instant chocolate pudding
- ☆ Milk
- ☆ Chocolate biscuits (we used bourbon creams!)
- ☆ Jelly snakes

## WHAT TO DO

✭ Follow the instructions on the pack to make the chocolate pudding.

✭ Once it has set, scoop it into a serving dish — the messier, the better!

✭ Put the biscuits into a food bag and bash them into crumbs with a rolling pin. Sprinkle the crumbs on top of the chocolate pudding so that it looks like dirt.

✭ To finish, arrange jelly worms on top of the dirt and eat!

# SPIDER SANDWICHES!

These crunchy sandwiches are super-scary!

## YOU WILL NEED

☆ Toast, cut into circles using a cookie cutter
☆ Peanut butter
☆ Jam
☆ Chocolate biscuit sticks
☆ Raisins
☆ White icing pen

*Mwah ha ha ha ha!*

## WHAT TO DO

✿ Spread the toast circles with peanut butter, then add a blob of jam in the middle — this will be a surprise filling for whoever you give one to! Put two together to make a sandwich.

✿ Slide in some chocolate biscuit sticks to make legs — remember, you need four on each side!

✿ Add a couple of raisins for eyes, sticking them on with peanut butter, then add a little white icing for the centres of the eyes!

✿ Now dare your friends to eat a spider sandwich!

29

# Beaker's Brilliant Birthday Cake!

## You will need:

- A round sponge cake
- A cocktail stick
- Cake frosting
- Red food colouring
- Black food colouring
- Liquorice laces
- A black icing pen

## It's totally tremendous!

**1** Use a cocktail stick to mark out the shape of Tracy's face. Don't worry about being too neat – this is just a guide for the next step!

**2** Add a few drops of red food colouring to your frosting to make a pale peach shade and carefully ice inside your markings for Tracy's face.

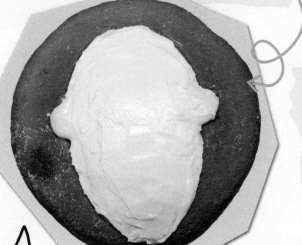

**3** Add some more red food colouring to your leftover frosting to darken it and add two dots for Tracy's cheeks.

**4** Add some black food colouring to your frosting and ice the rest of the cake – don't worry about being too neat as this will become Tracy's hair!

**5** Lay strips of liquorice laces over the black food colouring to make Tracy's hair – the wilder, the better!

**6** Finally, draw on Tracy's face with your icing pen.

**Tip!**
When creating Tracy's face, lightly mark where you want her eyes, nose and cheeks to go with a cocktail stick first.

Yum, yum!

# Party Perfect: Tracy Style!

**Get your party started with these super-fun games!**

## Character Call-out!

Sit in a circle and call out the names of JW characters as you go round. Each time someone repeats a character's name, they're out — the winner is the person who never repeats a name! Be super-swotty and name the books that they're in too if you can!

## Carry Those Coppers!

The object of this game is to get as many 1p and 2p coins from one end of the room and place them in a bowl at the other end... the catch is that you must transport them between your knees! Only coins that land in the bowl can be counted, and the winner is the player who collects the most coins during the course of the game!

## Pass The Sweet!

Sit in a circle and give everyone a plastic spoon which they hold between their lips or teeth by the handle. One person has a sweet placed on their spoon and the object of the game is to pass it around everyone without dropping it. If you drop the sweet, you're out — the person who never drops the sweet is the winner!

32

Sweets

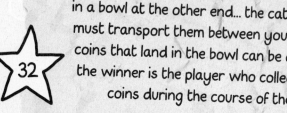

chocolate bar ←

yum! ↑

# Chocolate Chase!

For this game, you will need a large bar of chocolate, a knife and fork, a dice, a hat, a scarf, and a pair of gloves. Sit in a circle and put everything apart from the dice in the middle. Take it in turns to roll the dice — if you get a six you must go into the centre of the circle, put on the hat, scarf and gloves and try to eat as much of the chocolate as you can using the knife and fork. The other players keep rolling the dice until someone gets a six — then it's their turn to go to the centre of the circle and try to eat the chocolate! The one who finishes the bar is the winner!

## TIP!
Play your favourite song as a timer — when it ends, everyone must stop building!

# Toothpick Towers!

For this game, you'll need toothpicks and mini marshmallows. Work in teams to build the tallest tower using the toothpicks and marshmallows — the winner is the team whose tower is tallest (and still standing!) after the time is up!

# Do you Dare?

Fill a bag with loads of silly dares and take it in turns to pick one out and perform the task. Here are some to get you started!

Sing your favourite song in a funny voice!

Do your most embarrassing dance moves in front of everyone!

Wear your clothes back to front for the rest of the party!

Do star jumps until it's your next turn to pick a dare!

Tell everyone your funniest joke!

Get your friends to give you a crazy makeover, then pose for them as if you're a model!

For the next hour, if someone asks you a question with a yes or no answer, bark like a dog before you respond!

# Take The Tracy Test!

Are you the ultimate Beaker fan? Find out with these Tracy quiz cards!

## The Story Of Tracy Beaker

**1.** What does Tracy have to climb when she plays The Dare Game with Justine?

**2.** In Tracy's letter to Cam, who gobs all over the fairies at the bottom of the page?

**3.** What does Tracy have when she goes to McDonald's with Cam?

**4.** What did Tracy say her chat show would be called?

Answers:
1 A tree. 2 Goblinda the Goblin. 3. A Big Mac, French fries and a strawberry milkshake. 4. THE TRACY BEAKER EXPERIENCE.

## Starring Tracy Beaker

**1.** What part is Tracy given in the school play?

**2.** What meal does Mike bring Tracy on a tray?

**3.** What job do Mike and Jenny give Tracy as a punishment?

**4.** What activity do Cam and Tracy get up to on Christmas morning?

Answers:
1. Ebenezer Scrooge. 2. Spaghetti bolognese 3. Cleaning. 4. Ice-skating.

## The Dare Game

**1.** What are Cam's friends called?

**2.** What colour is Tracy's notebook?

**3.** Who does Tracy meet at her hideaway house?

**4.** What is Tracy dared to leave hanging on a tree?

Answers:
1 Jane and Liz. 2. Purple. 3. Alexander and Football 4. Her knickers.

## Tracy Beaker's Thumping Heart

**1.** What does Peter give Tracy as a Valentine's gift?

**2.** Who does Tracy have a crush on?

**3.** Who does Tracy gunge on Swap Shop?

**4.** What does Tracy try to win on Swap Shop?

Answers:
1 A heart-shaped locket. 2. Barney. 3. Justine Littlewood. 4 A karaoke kit.

Exclusive NEW short story!

# Tracy's Super-Star Birthday

Written by Jacqueline Wilson

Guess what? It's all about me!

Jenny

Justine

Peter

Read and Review!

Colour the stars to rate *Tracy's Super-Star Birthday*

What's the most important day of your life? It's obvious, isn't it? It's your *birthday*!

My birthday's on 8th May. I bet I had wonderful birthdays when I was little and Mum looked after me. She probably showered me with hundreds of dolls and teddies and cute little bunny outfits and my own tiny television to fix to the end of my cot and my own baby laptop with a lovely smiley photo of my mum as a screensaver. But then my mum couldn't look after me any more. I'm sure it wasn't her *fault*. She just got far too busy and successful being an actress in Hollywood, making film after film. She's still terribly in demand now. But she's going to take a break any time soon. She'll drive up to the Dumping Ground in her pink limo and I'll jump in and then we'll be off, Mum and me, and we'll live happily ever after and it'll be just *like* a movie.

But meanwhile I'm stuck in this rubbish Children's Home and my birthdays have gone rapidly down hill. *Especially* last year! This weedy little kid Peter had just ended up in the Dumping Ground and you will never ever believe this dire coincidence — his birthday is on 8th May too!

It was as if he'd come along deliberately to spoil my best day of the entire year. He shared all my special birthday treats. He got jam pancakes for breakfast as well as me. He got cards and presents — and some of his presents were exactly the same as mine. I had this enormous set of very select felt pens in all the colours of the rainbow and so did he! He got a special birthday party at the Dumping Ground too. Jenny crayoned a special banner saying Happy Birthday Tracy and Peter.

*Happy Birthday Tracy ~~and Peter~~*

I saw red when I spotted that banner. Still, I had my new set of felt pens. When everyone else was changing out of their school uniform I made a quick alteration. I shortened it a little by crossing out two superfluous words. The ones at the end.

When Jenny saw she was very cross.
'Really Tracy, do you have to be so mean to poor Peter?' she said. 'He'll be so upset when he sees his name crossed off the banner.'

'Call yourself a careworker! You're not meant to say we're mean. You're meant to understand that we're unhappy or angry or insecure!' I snapped. 'And I wasn't being *mean* anyway. I was simply trying out my new red felt pen to see if it worked properly.'

I nearly ended up being banned from my own birthday party! And guess what — I had to share my birthday cake! Every child in the Dumping Ground gets their very own iced cake on their birthday. You'd have thought the very least they could do was give Peter and me a cake each. I mean, that's *fair*, isn't it? But no, we had to share the lousy cake, and that meant we had to blow out the candles together and cut the first slice holding the same knife. That's when you make your birthday wish. But sharing the cake and the candles and the knife meant I had to share the wish with Peter too.

It was only *half* a wish, so it didn't come true. My mum didn't come and see me.

Still, that was *last* year. I was determined my next birthday was going to be different. It was going to be the best birthday ever and I wasn't going to let weedy little Peter spoil it. I wasn't sure *how* I was going to make it happen — until I started browsing through a *Starz!* magazine. Elaine the Pain, my social worker, lends all her old mags to

Jenny. I like to look in them too, just in case I catch a glimpse of my mum. I sometimes cut out pictures of the prettiest ladies, the ones with lots of blonde hair and gorgeous designer clothes and amazing high heels, and stick them on my walls. I tell the other kids they're all photos of my mum. Well, they *could* be.

I was flicking through the pages, looking for blonde look–alikes, when I saw the words *Super–Star Birthday Competition!* My hands started shaking as I read. I couldn't believe it. *Starz!* was quite a new celebrity mag. It started up last May — and to celebrate its first birthday it was running the most fantastic competition ever. The winner would get a super–star birthday day out as a prize, to share with a special friend. You'd get driven to this ultra posh hotel in London in a pink limo (just like my mum's!) and then you'd have a fancy lunch with all the magazine people, with an amazing cake specially designed for you by the head chef. A cake all of your own. No sharing!

**Starz!** Celebs, Celebs, Celebs

*Super–Star Birthday Competition*

Then there'd be a special makeover, and a new wardrobe of designer clothes, and they'd do a special photo feature in the magazine. Oh, I badly wanted a makeover! When I was little I used to be cute, all over curls with rosy cheeks and a cheeky smile. My mum thought the world of me then. But I seem to have gone off a bit as I've got older. My hair's just this wild frizz no matter how I brush it, and I'm pale and I don't really do smiling much anymore. My mouth seems to want to scowl instead.

I really really really needed that makeover. Then my mum would feel so proud of me she'd want me with her all the time, no matter how busy she was. I *had* to win the competition!

You had to write in and say *why* you wanted a super-star birthday celebration. Well, that was easy enough! I could write pages and pages explaining *exactly* why. And I'd go on and on about being a poor little looked-after child in the care system, with no decent clothes and hardly any toys, and they'd feel so sorry for me they'd surely let me win!

I went rushing off to use the ropey old computer in our living room. Little Wayne was messing around on it, which was seriously bad news. Wayne is one of those kids who always has a runny nose and sticky fingers. He was actually eating a Krispy Kreme doughnut and jam was leaking out all over the keyboard!

'Yuck! Go and wash, you mucky little boy,' I said, pushing him off the chair. I tried scrubbing at the keyboard with a tissue, to no avail. Wayne started crying because he'd dropped his doughnut when I pushed him. It wasn't really my fault. He shouldn't have been sitting at the computer in the first place. I nearly burst into tears of frustration too — though of course I never ever cry. I might suffer from a little hay fever every now and then, but that's not an emotional weakness, it's a medical condition.

'Don't cry, Wayne,' said weedy little Peter, picking up his doughnut and inspecting it. 'It's only a *little* bit dusty. I'm sure you can still eat the jammy part in the middle.

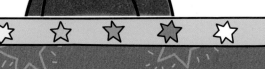

Now stop that silly crying. You're annoying my friend Tracy.'

'I'm not *your* friend!' I said, glaring at him. As if I'd ever want a little twerp like Peter Ingham as my friend! He thought he could muscle in and make friends with me just because my true best friend Louise had betrayed me horrendously and gone off with my worst enemy, Justine Littlewood.

'I wish we *were* friends, Tracy,' said Peter wistfully, looking at me with his big Bambi eyes.

I think Peter looks a total weed, and so would anyone with any sense — but he's the sort of big-eyed blonde curly-haired boy that makes old ladies start drooling and calling him a little pet. He'll get fostered in no time, it's obvious.

'What do you want to write on the computer, Tracy?' he asked.

'It's a secret. Push off!' I said, trying to make the jammy keys work properly. Peter took a couple of steps backwards but still hovered. I did my best to ignore him and got into the flow of my competition entry.

'Are you writing a story, Tracy?' Peter asked. 'I love your stories.'

'No! Now scram, go on.'

He retreated to the sofa and hunched up in a corner, still watching me intently. He saw me refer to the magazine article, checking on all the details.

'Are you writing a piece for the magazine all about super-stars?' Peter asked excitedly. 'Oh Tracy, are you writing about your famous mum?'

Justine Littlewood happened to be sauntering down the corridor and snorted loudly.

'Tracy Beaker's mum isn't *famous*, you idiot,' she said.

'Yes, she is! She's a film star and one day soon she's going to come for Tracy and they'll live in Hollywood and make films together,' said Peter.

'You are *soooo* stupid, Peter. Tracy's been filling you up with a lot of rubbish. Her mum's never ever going to come,' said Justine.

She raised her voice, to make sure I heard. She waited for me to lose it and attack her. But just this once I wasn't going to be goaded. I needed to concentrate on my competition entry and get it in on time. And then when I won I'd invite my mum along as my special friend. She loved posh meals and fancy hotels and she'd jump at the chance of designer clothes and a makeover. She wouldn't be able to resist, even if she was right in the middle of making a movie. She'd come running and we'd have the best birthday day out *ever*!

So I carried on tap tap tapping on the jammy computer, telling the magazine just how much it would mean to me to win the competition.

*"It would be so wonderful to have a really special birthday treat just for me. When you're in a care home you always have to share. Please please please let me be the winner!"*

There! I checked the magazine again for the right e-mail address. I was so absorbed I'd forgotten all about Peter. He suddenly bobbed up by my side, peering at the magazine too.

'Oh Tracy, you're going in for a competition!' he said.

'No, I'm not!' I said quickly, trying to snatch the magazine back.

'It's a special birthday competition! Oh wow, you get to ride in a stretch limo and go to a fancy hotel — and you can take a friend!' Peter burbled. 'I'm going to go in for this competition too, and if I win I'll take you, Tracy, and we'll have the best birthday ever!'

*'I'm going to win, not you!'* I said.

'You're not *either* of you going to win,' said Justine, grabbing the magazine herself. 'You're crazy! This isn't a kids'

competition. This is for adults. You'll never win in a million years, Tracy Beaker.'

'Yes I will, just you wait and see!' I said, pressing the little 'send' image. I imagined my competition entry flying through the air and pinging into the magazine editor's computer. I saw her reading it, a big smile spreading across her face. I felt a smile spreading over *my* face too.

'Look at her! She's on Planet Fairyland!' Justine sneered.

*Yes, and it's a wonder I didn't sprout wings and sprinkle fairy dust, because you'll never ever guess what. I did win! I really did, even though it was an adult competition and they had thousands of entries!*

Traceeeeee!' Jenny yelled. 'What's all this about entering a competition? You know perfectly well you should ask my permission first!'

'Jeneeeee!' I yelled back. 'What's all this about reading other people's emails? You know perfectly well you should ask my permission first!'

*Jenny would normally tell me off for cheeking her — but she came charging out of* her office and gave me a great big hug!

'You've only gone and won!' she said. 'Oh, you're such a crazy kid. Whatever are you going to do next?' I was so dumbfounded I stood stock still for a moment, speechless. But the Beaker is never at a loss for long.

'I've WON!' I shouted, and I ran up and down the entire Dumping Ground, yelling the good news to everyone. Oh, you should have seen Justine Littlewood's face! It was one of the most glorious moments of my life. But I was going to have an entire glorious *day*.

'A ride in a limo, a meal at the hotel, then a makeover,' Jenny read out, bemused. 'Hey, why didn't I go in for this competition myself? It says you can choose a friend to take with you! Who are you going to take, Tracy?'

'Well, I'm not taking you, Jenny, so don't get your hopes up,' I said.

'I think *someone* will have to come with you from the Home, chickie — but I'm sure you can take a friend too. And I've just had a lovely idea!' said Jenny.

'What?' I saw she was looking in weedy Peter's direction. 'No way!' I said firmly. 'Peter's so not not not my friend. I'm not taking him, not in a million years.'

'Tracy! Keep your voice down! You'll hurt Peter's feelings,' said Jenny.

Peter

Justine

'Are you sure I can't persuade you? It's Peter's birthday too. It would be lovely to share your super-star day out with him.'

'Tracy Beaker doesn't do sharing,' I said. 'And I can't take Peter, even if I liked him. I'm taking my best friend ever.'

'Is that *me*?' said Louise, suddenly all smiles, even though she'd barely spoken to me for weeks.

'No, it is *not* you!' I said.

'How about taking me, Beaker?' said Justine Littlewood. She really said it!

'You just happen to be my worst enemy, Justine Littlewood. Of course I'm not taking you,' I said.

This was getting to be highly enjoyable!

'So who *are* you taking, Tracy?' asked Jenny.

'She can't take anyone, because she hasn't *got* anyone who wants to be her friend,' said Justine.

'I have so! I've got heaps of friends,' I said.

'She's got me. I'm her friend,' said Peter, in his little mouse-squeak. 'But it's okay, Tracy, I know you don't want to take me *too*. You'll want to take your mum, won't you?'

Peter Ingham is so irritating! He's too good at guessing.

'Oh Tracy,' said Jenny. 'It's a lovely idea, but I'm not quite sure your mum will be able to make it. She's been out of touch recently.'

'Well, let's get her back *in* touch. You write to her, Jenny! If you tell her all about the competition, and the makeover and the designer clothes, she'll come, I just know she will,' I said.

I wrote to Mum too. I wrote pages and pages and pages. And then I added a final page with *Please Come* in fancy silver lettering (I borrowed Justine's new pen when they were having a nail–painting session in Louise's room) and then I filled the rest of the space with stars and squiggles and *hundreds* of kisses.

'That looks simply beautiful, Tracy,' said Peter.

'Why do you have to be such a creep all the time?' I said.

'I don't know. I'm sorry. I didn't *mean* to be a creep,' said Peter, and he slunk away.

I had a tight feeling in my chest and a squeezy feeling in my stomach then. I often got it when I'd been talking to weedy Peter. I decided the remedy was simple. I'd avoid him at all costs.

I also found I had to avoid Justine too, because she discovered her special silver pen was all used up, and she decided for no reason at all that I was the chief suspect.

Still, I didn't care about trivial little skirmishes with the stupid kids in the Dumping Ground. I was going to have my super–star birthday outing with my mum. Nothing else mattered.

The magazine got in touch with Jenny to finalize details for the Big Day. I was a little annoyed, as it wasn't *Jenny*'s big day, but she had to give her permission, acting like my parent.

'I've *got* a parent! My mum! She'll be coming with me,' I protested.

'Yes, I know that's what you're hoping, Tracy, but we haven't heard from your mum yet. It might not work out quite the way you want. And if she can't make it for any reason, then —'

'She'll make it!'

'Tracy, I've tried writing to her and phoning her. Several times.'

'Let me phone her! You're not telling her properly,' I wailed. It's so unfair. She's my mum, yet I'm not allowed to phone her or know her address.

'I've done my best, Tracy,' Jenny said gently.

'Then it's not good enough!' I shouted. 'But she *will* come, she will, she will, she will!'

I started to get seriously angry and went into one of my royal strops and had to be put in the Quiet Room for a while. I made a lot of noise in the Quiet Room for some considerable time. I didn't *cry*, I never ever cry, but somehow I ended up with very sore eyes and hiccups. I waited for weedy Peter to come sidling into the room. He usually lends me one of his nan's hankies at such times, and a soothing fruit drop.

He didn't come near me this time. Of course I was glad. I mean, who wants that weedy little creep hanging round all the time?

I made a determined effort not to get down-hearted. I'd won the super-star birthday treat and my mum was going to enjoy it with me, *I knew* it. I wrote her another letter. And another. And another.

'Are you *sure* you're sending them to the right address, Jenny?' I said accusingly.

Perhaps it was all *her* fault? Or perhaps my mum had moved somewhere else entirely? Or maybe she was ill and couldn't reply? Or maybe she was on location making a movie?

She didn't get in touch till the 8th May — my actual birthday. I was up in my room, dealing with a sudden terrible attack of hay-fever, not even feeling like coming downstairs and eating birthday pancakes for breakfast.

'Happy birthday, Tracy!' said Jenny, holding out a parcel. 'I think it's from your mum!'

I tore the parcel open. There was a birthday card and a present.

I read the message inside the card —

Dear Tracy,
Have a really great super-star birthday, babe! So sorry can't make it – I'm seeing Uncle Charlie and we're staying at his place.
Hope you like the present! Party party party!
Lots of love,
Mum
XXX

'She's not coming. She's seeing Uncle Charlie,' I said to Jenny.
'I didn't know you had an Uncle Charlie, Tracy,' said Jenny.

'Neither did I. I can't stick all Mum's uncles,' I said, unwrapping my present.

*It was a pair of shiny silver shoes with real heels!*

'Oh my goodness!' said Jenny.

'Wow! Real grown up high heels!' I said, trying them on. They were quite tight. Very very tight, in fact. Perhaps they were a little bit too small. Several sizes, in fact. Mum always forgets I keep growing. But I kept them proudly on my feet.

'Just wait till Justine and Louise see my party shoes with real heels!' I said.

'That's the spirit,' said Jenny. 'So — who are you taking for your super—star birthday outing now?'

'I don't know.' Jenny had that look on her face. '*Definitely* not Peter Ingham,' I said firmly.

'You know Peter went in for the competition too?' said Jenny.

'Yes, but he didn't win. *I* did,' I said, practicing walking in my silver shoes. I was a bit wobbly.

'I read Peter's entry. He said he was desperate to win the competition because he knew how much his friend Tracy wanted to have a ride in a stretch limo and a meal in a hotel and a makeover,' said Jenny.

I started to feel wobbly all over.

'I'm not his friend,' I mumbled. 'Anyway, I don't think he likes me any more, not since I called him a creep.'

'Oh Tracy! I think he still likes you very very much. He's got a birthday card for you. Come downstairs and see it,' said Jenny.

I went downstairs, wincing and mincing in my shoes. Louise and Justine squealed enviously when they saw them. Everyone started singing *Happy Birthday* and Mike started making the pancakes.

I had three cards. One was a big funny one, and all the kids in the Dumping Ground had signed it. There was a red smear of jam beside Wayne's name. There was another card from Mike and Jenny. And a third card, home—made, very long and thin. It was a picture of a long wriggly worm squiggling through lots of blades of grass, but it had Peter's face, with his big eyes and fair curls. It had a speech bubble above its little Peter head. *Happy Birthday, Tracy. I can't help being a creep! Love from Peter.*

Peter smiled at me anxiously. He was sitting all hunched up with his head bent.

He only had two cards, one from the kids, and one from Mike and Jenny.

I had that tight feeling in my chest and a squeezing feeling in my tummy again. So tight and squeezy I could scarcely breathe.

    'Just a tick,' I said, hobbling out the kitchen in my high heels.

    'Tracy! I'm making you a pancake!' Mike called.

    'Yeah, yeah, I'm only going to be a minute,' I said. I snatched a piece of paper and someone's pen. I wrote: *Happy Birthday little wormy boy. Want to come on my special super-star birthday trip? You'd better say yes! Tracy.*

He did say yes. He said *yes-yes-yes-yes-yes!* The pink stretch limo came and picked us up at eleven o'clock. All the kids crowded out of the Dumping Ground to watch us get in. The chauffeur let everyone pile in together and be driven round the block. But then they all had to get out, and Peter and Jenny and I got in and were driven off in style.

It was amazing! The windows were blacked out, but we could still see out, and watch everyone staring at us. We pulled the most terrible faces at everyone! Then the chauffeur played some music and we sang along. Jenny and the chauffeur sang too!

Then we got to the posh hotel and the magazine people were there to meet us, treating us like royalty. The hotel was *soooo* shiny and grand that even Jenny came over all shy, but I strutted about in my silver shoes and smiled as if I were a real movie star like my mum. We were led up to our special suite where lunch was served — and you'll never ever guess what! We had our very own butler! He was called Nick and he kept offering us drinks and food, and he called me Miss Tracy! Jenny kept fluttering her eyelashes at him, and whispered that she'd like to take him home with her.

We sat down at a specially laid table with a snowy white cloth. I kicked off my silver shoes because no-one could see under the table. My toes had such a happy wriggle to be free at last.

I was a bit worried that the food might be very strange and fancy and almost too posh, but it was lovely little bits of

**Happy birthday Tracy. I can't help being a creep! Love from Peter.**

chicken and really crispy chips, with our own little bowls of tomato sauce. Then there was a fruit salad with ice cream, and *then* there was a big pink birthday cake.

'Do you want to blow out the candles and cut the cake with me, seeing as it's your birthday too, Peter?' I said.

'Yes please, Tracy — but you can have my wish,' said Peter. '*My* wish has already come true!'

Then we went into the big bedroom for our makeover. The stylist straightened my hair so it wasn't all frizzy and put a little bit of make up on my face, so that my cheeks were pink and my eyes looked sparkly. Then I got to try on all these different incredible outfits. I'd left my silver shoes under the table but it didn't matter. They'd checked my shoe size with Jenny, and had all sorts of different patent pumps and scarlet Converse boots and crazy flowery sneakers to go with each outfit.

They took heaps of photos of me to go in the magazine. Some of them were me on my own, but some were with Peter.

When the magazine came out there was a caption under the main photo of Peter and me holding hands and grinning.

*Here's our little super—star birthday girl Tracy with her friend Peter on her special day out.*

I gave Peter his own copy of the magazine, and I underlined the word *friend*.

I don't know what's the matter with me. I seem to have had a makeover inside as well as out. I took the remains of my birthday cake back with me and shared it round all the kids in the Dumping Ground. I even gave a slice to Justine Littlewood!!!

Here's our little super—star birthday girl Tracy with her friend Peter on her special day out.

# Create A Goodie!
## The Tracy Beaker Way!

Hi sister writers! Pay attention while I teach you how to create a good character for a story...

Peter

○ Introduce your character by writing an interesting paragraph about them. Use loads of descriptive words to show how amazing they are. Here's an example I've written — it's about me because I'm the greatest but you can invent someone more ordinary!

☆ Show how brave and brilliant your character is. Write about how they've helped a friend out of a sticky situation. Remember how I helped Alexander when he broke his leg in *The Dare Game*? Or when I gave sniffly Peter his locket back in *Tracy Beaker's Thumping Heart*?

☆ It was obvious from an early age that Tracy Beaker was going to be famous. She was super-cool from the start and we could tell that she was extra-special. Poor little Tracy had a tragic life but when her mum, who was so-o-o glamorous, whisked her off to Hollywood, everything changed for the better. Tracy got 10 out of 10 for writing at her new Hollywood school and everyone knew that she would become a best-selling author.

○ Now write a paragraph about your goodie here:

---------------------------------------

---------------------------------------

---------------------------------------

---------------------------------------

burger → yum

dream house

⭐ Make your character real by writing a few scenes from their point of view. Are they chatty? Do they love to dress up or are they super—scruffy (like Cam!)? What foods do they like? What sort of house do they live in? Do they have any pets?

⭐ Every character needs a stand—out feature — something they say all the time or a nervous habit they have. Decide what yours will be. Then your terrific character will really come to life!

⭕ It's a great idea to sketch what your character looks like. Draw your perfect goodie here!

⭐ As we all know, not even the wonderful Tracy Beaker is good all the time. Even a tip top person like me has faults so, even though your character is good, they will have flaws and might even shout and scream at times!

⭕ Don't forget to give your character an amazing name to match their terrific personality. Keep all this info strictly private until your story is finished!

Triple Gold Star!

Champion Tracy

Check out my totally brilliant tips for creating a baddie!

# Beaker's Baddies!

Justine

○ The baddie in my life is obviously Justine–Clown–Face–Littlewood, but adults take one look at her and think she's an angel — it's so annoying! Sometimes real baddies don't look as mean as they actually are. Decide if your character is going to look super–scary, or if their appearance is deceiving!

○ It's so much fun creating a baddie for your stories, so let your imagination run wild. Rule number one: baddies are never boring! Jot down a r–e–a–l–l–y crazy thing that your baddie has done in the past...

------------------------------

------------------------------

------------------------------

------------------------------

☆ When I watch films, my favourite characters are always the baddies — they're much more exciting than some boring goodie–two–shoes. I especially love when baddies have their very own catchphrase — something they say all the time. Try and come up with one for your character here...

Black belt Tracy

50

⭐ Baddies usually have a reason for being so mean. I reckon Justine is only rude to me because she's insanely jealous of my talent and good looks, for example. Think about why your character acts the way they do... Maybe something really bad happened to them a long time ago!

⭕ Some baddies have no friends, while others have a gang of equally-horrible mates they hang around with. What about your character? Are they a bit of a loner, or are they annoyingly popular? Do they have any family, and if so, are they just as mean?

⭕ It's a great idea to sketch what your character looks like. Draw your best baddie here!

⭐ One of the most important features of any character is their name. Bad people sometimes have scary or mean-sounding names, but maybe your villain actually has a sweet, sensitive name which fools people! Write your character's name below:

⭐ While baddies are always mean, some things really make their blood boil. Justine gets especially angry when I mention her stupid dad. What causes your villain to really show their dark side?

51

# The Tracy Beaker Outrageous Dare Challenge!

## How to play:

⭐ Colour the stars to rate each dare.

⭐ Now tick the box to say whether you could ever do this dare or not.

⭐ Totally — 3
⭐ Maybe — 2
⭐ No way! — 1

## Totally Tracy!

The Tremendous Tracy Beaker sticks her tongue out at Mrs Bagley...

**Dare rating!** ⭐⭐⭐⭐☆

**Could you do this dare?**

Totally! ☐ Maybe ☐ No way! ☐

## Wicked Words!

Justine-Too-Annoying-For-Words Littlewood makes the vicar blush when she says bad words...

**Dare rating!** ⭐⭐⭐☆☆

**Could you do this dare?**

Totally! ☐ Maybe ☐ No way! ☐

**Totally Starkers!**
Tracy Beaker streaks naked through the garden...
**Dare rating!** ★★☆★★☆
**Could you do this dare?**
Totally! ☐ Maybe ☐ No way! ☐

**Rude Roxanne**
Roxanne says something very rude indeed to Mrs Bagley...
**Dare rating!** ★★★★★☆
**Could you do this dare?**
Totally! ☐ Maybe ☐ No way! ☐

**Wriggly Worm**
Justine–Hideous–Face–Littlewood eats two worms...
**Dare rating!** ★★★☆★☆
**Could you do this dare?**
Totally! ☐ Maybe ☐ No way! ☐

**Tree Trauma!**
The Fearless Tracy Beaker climbs the highest tree...
**Dare rating!** ★★★★☆☆
**Could you do this dare?**
Totally! ☐ Maybe ☐ No way! ☐

## Spaghetti Shame

Tracy the Great tips spaghetti over her own head then over Roxanne's...

**Dare rating!** ✩✩✩✩✩

**Could you do this dare?**

Totally! ☐  Maybe ☐  No way! ☐

## Assault Course!

Justine Pain–In–The–Neck–Littlewood completes the Tracy Beaker Skateboard Challenge...

**Dare rating!** ✩✩✩✩✩

**Could you do this dare?**

Totally! ☐  Maybe ☐  No way! ☐

## Now add up your scores to find your Daredevil Rating!

**1-8** Mmmm, you may have been hanging out with sniffly cry–baby Peter. You need to take some Daredevil lessons from the amazing, incredible Tracy Beaker!

**9-16** You can take up a challenge but, just like Justine– Pain–In–The–Neck–Littlewood, you're not quite as splendiferously Daredevilish as the Tremendous Tracy Beaker!

**17-24** You're a true Daredevil, Tracy Beaker style. You could take up any challenge and call it easy–peasy!

# Dastardly 8

## Peter

☆ He's snivelly, soppy, creepy, weirdy... need I go on?

☆ He always looks like he's going to burst into tears over his stupid nan!

☆ He follows me around ALL THE TIME!

☆ He thinks I'm his best friend. Well, guess what, Peetie—Weetie... I'M NOT!

0     5     10

## Louise

✦ She's a TRAITOR!

✦ She's annoying, annoying, ANNOYING!

✦ She puts on this stupid little angel act and has the world's most squeaky voice!

✦ She told my night—time secret to Justine Pea—brain Littlewood!

0     5     10

56

# Deadly Enemies!

## Elaine
*The pain!!!*

⭐ She's ultra-bossy!

⭐ Her bum wobble, wobble, wobbles when she walks!

⭐ She always uses stupid social worker speak — apparently I'm "challenging" (that means "difficult")!

⭐ She never lets me visit my mum on the Hollywood sets of her movies! My mum's a famous actress, don't you know?

 0 ———— 5 ———— 10

## Justine
Bottom-face Littlewood!

☆ She gunged me live on TV!

☆ She's a snivelling, sneaky tell-tale!

☆ She has absolutely no discernable talent whatsoever, unlike me, the ultra-talented Tracy Beaker!

☆ She STOLE my best friend!

*11!*

0 ———— 5 ———— 1̶0̶

# Tracy-Tastic Door Sign!

Keep out the riff-raff with this easy-peasy idea!

**You'll Need:**
* Card — recycle an old box
* Wrapping paper
* Plain paper and pen
* Glue stick
* String or ribbon
* Sticky tape

⭐ Cut out a square of card and cover it with your chosen wrapping paper.

⭐ Draw a picture for your sign on plain paper. I chose a scary skull and crossbones design, you can trace it if you like.

⭐ Now write BOG OFF! in big letters. Cut out the letters and picture and glue them to your card.

⭐ Finish by taping a piece of string to the back. Hang on your door to keep pesky intruders (Justine, you know who I mean!) at bay.

BOG OFF!

100% private

Why not...

... add an extra warning? Here are some ideas —
* 100% Private
* No Peeking!
* Enter At Your Peril!
* Beaker Besties ONLY!
* Private Property!

... add some sparkly stickers or glitter too?

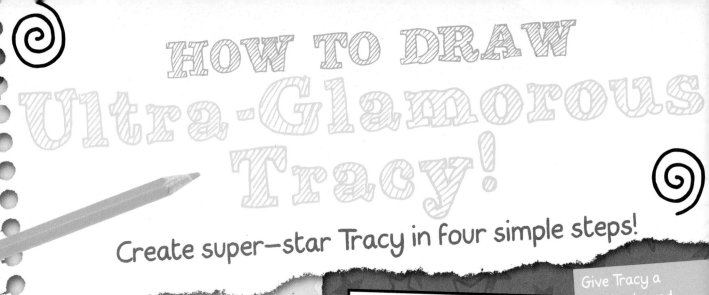

# HOW TO DRAW
## Ultra-Glamorous Tracy!

Create super–star Tracy in four simple steps!

**1**

Begin by drawing Tracy's newly–straightened hair and the shape of her head. Add her neck and draw curved lines for her necklaces.

**2**

Give Tracy a short–sleeved dress and draw a belt round her middle. Draw one arm in pen and the other in pencil — you will have to ad detail to this arm i the next step.

**3**

Draw a little handbag and a chunky bracelet on Tracy's arm before inking in her arm and adding her legs. Give Tracy a pair of ankle–length boots.

**4**

Fill in Tracy's face, giving her a big lipsticky smile and blushed cheeks. Now use your brightest colours to design a funky outfit for Tracy — we've given her cool Converse boots, stripy tights and a skull–patterned dress

60

# Draw Tracy here! ↘

**Nick's Tip!**
Use a gold pen to draw Tracy's necklaces — it really makes them stand out!

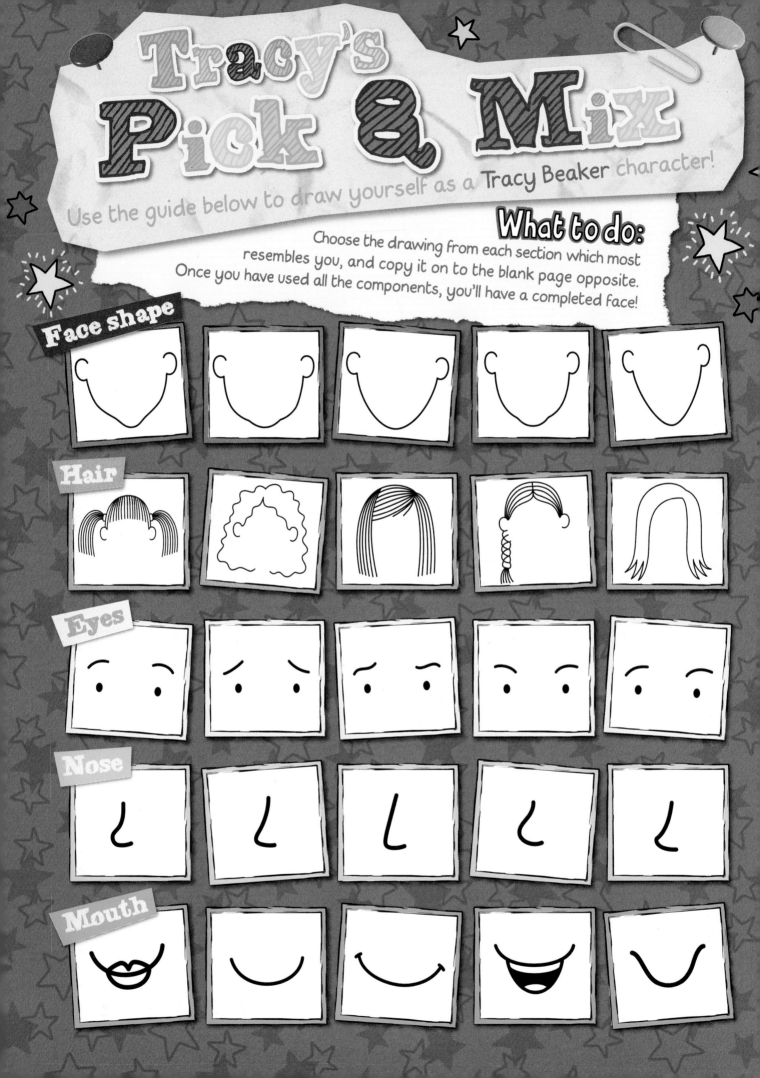

**Tip!** Sketch your character in pencil first then finalise in pen!

63

# Beaker's Brainstorm!

Adele

Louise

Cam

Mike

## Wordsearch!

Can you find these Tracy Beaker characters in the grid below?

```
X E X G C L S J M K N W E
V H A F M J B K C C K G L
D B H V U Q A J V C K Y A
R E T E P G M G D O N T I
O B V E J O Y E O N D L N
J F E J O I L G N T L E Z
Y G F J U U G E J U I S C
H M E I E T J D O Z T T Z
O S A O N A T C H M C A D
E R U X T Y X E D O X D C
M I K E Y E A Y N C E A M
H M C M A V U W O E L P J
T I O X C B E X Q Z Z A Y
```

Peter

Elaine

## True or False?

1. Cam used M&Ms to decorate Tracy's birthday cake with her initials. ☐T ☐F

2. Tray's imaginary chat show is called *The Tracy Beaker Experience.* ☐T ☐F

3. Tracy was once fostered by a couple called Aunt Meggy and Uncle Tim. ☐T ☐F

4. Cam's surname is Lawton. ☐T ☐F

5. Cam's car is green. ☐T ☐F

Justine

Jenny

Wayne

Maxy

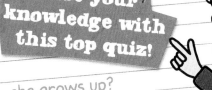

# Are You A Tracy Beaker Know-it-all?!

**Test your knowledge with this top quiz!**

Justine

1. What does Tracy hate eating?
2. When is Tracy's birthday?
3. What is Tracy's lucky number?
4. What does Tracy want to be when she grows up?
5. What did Tracy notice that Cam has on her socks?
6. What does Tracy give to Justine at the end of *The Story of Tracy Beaker*?
7. What's Cam's address?
8. What's Justine's surname?
9. What are the names of the couple who fostered Tracy before they had a baby of their own?
10. What's Tracy's favourite colour?

urger

yum!

## What's Changed?

Jacqueline Wilson
The Story of Tracy Beaker
Illustrated by Nick Sharratt

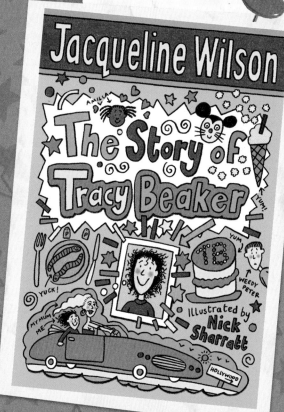

Jacqueline Wilson
The Story of Tracy Beaker
Illustrated by Nick Sharratt

There are six differences between the book covers — can you spot them?

65

**ANSWERS:**

**True or False: 1.** False - She used Smarties **2.** True **3.** False - They were called Aunt Peggy and Uncle Sid **4.** False - It's Lawson **5.** True **6.** May 8 **7.** An Author. **8.** Books **6.** Her Mickey Mouse pen **7.** 10 Beech Road, Kingtown **8.** Julie and Ted **10.** Blood-red **What's Changed? 1.** Spelling of 'CAMILLA' changed to 'AMILLA' **2.** One flake removed from ice cream. **3.** Colour of ice cream changed. **4.** 'S' on salt shaker changed to 'P'. **5.** Colour of cake filling changed **6.** One of Tracy's mums earrings missing.

**Are You A Tracy Beaker Know-it-all?:**

# You're A Star!

Give your best photos the Tracy treatment with this easy-peasy frame!

**1.** Trace the star shape and cut a pattern from paper. Draw round it on to your card and cut out two stars.

**2.** Ask an adult to help you cut out the rectangle from <u>one</u> of the stars

**3.** Cover one star with tin foil. We've painted our other star, but you could cover this one in foil, too!

**4.** Now glue your photo in the bottom of the star and then stick the other star on top.

**Tip!** Use glitter pens to bling up your frame!

**5.** Finish by attaching a paper clip hanger to the back using glue or sticky tape. Hang it up and admire your handiwork!

# Super-slurpy Strawberry Sundaes!

**WARNING: This recipe is totally tasty!**

## You'll Need

*Serves roughly four people.*

- ⭐ 1 packet of strawberry jelly
- ⭐ 1 tub of ice cream of your choice (strawberry, vanilla or raspberry ripple are extra-tasty!)
- ⭐ A punnet of strawberries
- ⭐ A packet of ice cream wafers
- ⭐ A can of squirty cream

You can also add chopped nuts, sprinkles or chocolate chips if you want!

1. Make up your jelly according to the instructions on the packet. You'll need boiling water for this, so it's best to get an adult to give you a hand!

2. Chop up about 20 strawberries into quarters, and stir them into your jelly mixture before it sets.

3. Split this mixture between four sundae glasses and pop into the fridge until they've set. Make sure you only fill each one about half way.

4. When the mixture is ready, top it with some more chopped strawberries, two scoops of ice cream and some squirty cream, before finishing off with the ice cream wafers!

You can try using other fruits too. Banana sundaes are tremendously tasty!

# Totally Tall Tales!

**Play this fun game to make up a silly story about Tracy!**

## How to play:

Roll a dice to pick a sentence from each section. So, if you roll a six, you would select sentence number six. It's easy-peasy! When you've picked them all, read them out in order to hear your silly story!

### A — Start here!

## This morning, I was woken up by...

1. a big seagull tapping on my window!
2. Justine Littlewood barging into my bedroom!
3. a scary nightmare about giant bees!
4. my hair tickling my chin.
5. a clown giggling in my ear!
6. the smell of birthday cake wafting under my door.

*yum!*

*birthday cake*

### B

## So I decided to...

1. run downstairs immediately!
2. jump out of bed and do a crazy dance!
3. scream at the top of my lungs!
4. throw my duvet out the window!
5. hide behind my curtains!
6. drink a great big milkshake for breakfast!

*milkshake*

## C Then I went outside and saw...

1. a big, bouncy castle covered in strawberry jelly!
2. a dog the size of a horse!
3. a film crew making a Hollywood movie!
4. a witch fly past on a broomstick!
5. a life-sized gingerbread man walking down the street!
6. a pink sports car filled with balloons!

GRRR!

## D So I...

1. ran round in circles until I was dizzy!
2. wrote a letter to the Queen about what I'd seen!
3. caught the next bus into town.
4. climbed the highest tree I could find
5. painted pink polka-dots all over my face!
6. drank a whole jug of custard!

## E Then I heard that...

1. a casting director wanted me to be in his movie!
2. a tiger had escaped from the zoo!
3. a huge party was happening down the road!
4. chocolate sauce was coming out of the taps instead of water!
5. someone had cast a magic spell on me!
6. I had a secret twin sister!

## F So I...

1. laughed so much, my cheeks turned purple!
2. decided it had been the best day ever!
3. couldn't believe my luck!
4. made three wishes!
5. sang a song about sausages!
6. couldn't wait to tell my friends!

Try making up your own choices for even more laughs!

# Tracy's ~~Jacky's~~ Story School

I shouldn't really be sharing my best writing tips, but seeing as I'm such a nice person...

I love writing — it's ever so easy, you know. As long as you've got paper and a pen, anyone can give it a go. My favourite thing to write about is me. Who wouldn't want to read about the incredible Tracy Beaker? I'm intelligent, witty, creative and a whole lot of fun. Write down five things that are great about you — there's no room for modesty here!

1. ................................................................
2. ................................................................
3. ................................................................
4. ................................................................
5. ................................................................

felt tips

Writing about yourself is always a good place to start — even if you reckon your life is a bit of a bore-a-thon and Terrifically Unglamorous. Hey, my best-seller was set in The Dumping Ground! Plus, don't forget there's definitely nothing wrong with s–t–r–e–t–c–h–i–n–g the truth sometimes...

I'm especially brilliant at using descriptive words when I'm writing. You know — words that help me explain just how stupid Justine Pea–brain Littlewood is, or how breathtakingly beautiful my mum is, or how mouth–wateringly delicious that slice of birthday cake was. Mmm... I love writing about food. What's your favourite meal of all time? Describe it in the box on the opposite page.

birthday cake

yum!

**Favourite Meal**
**Top Tip:** it should make you drool when you read it back.

..............................................
..............................................
..............................................
..............................................

Now I want to find out more about you, so answer the rest of my questions. Remember, I'm extra–nosey, so don't hold back.

What's your bedroom like?

..............................................
..............................................
..............................................

What do you look like?

..............................................
..............................................
..............................................

If you had three wishes, what would you ask for and why?

..............................................
..............................................
..............................................

# Starring

..............................................

If you're going to make YOU the star of your story, it's time to think about the things you definitely don't want to leave out. Fill in the gaps below to get you started.

⭐ **I'm happiest when...**

..............................................
..............................................

⭐ **My favourite friend is..**

..............................................
..............................................

⭐ **Someone who always cheers me up is...**

..............................................
..............................................

⭐ **My best day ever was..**

..............................................
..............................................

⭐ **My saddest day ever was..**

..............................................
..............................................

⭐ **The best thing about my life is..**

..............................................
..............................................

# Tracy Truth OR Beaker OR Bluff?

Test your friends!

## Sort out Tracy's fibs from the facts!

**1.** Just occasionally I might 'borrow' Justine's makeup. Like when Cam came to visit. Well, I wanted to look my best, didn't I?

○ FACT OR ○ FIB

**2.** Mike wasn't too impressed when he had to rescue me from the roof of the Dumping Ground after I completed a Perilous and Extremely Hazardous dare — spoilsport!

○ FACT OR ○ FIB

**3.** My new friend Alexander was so upset when the other kids at his school started calling him Gherkin.

○ FACT OR ○ FIB

**4.** I completely wowed the audience with my Incredibly Inspirational performance as the Ghost of Christmas Past in the school production of A Christmas Carol.

○ FACT OR ○ FIB

HURRAY!

THE GREATEST PERFORMANCE EVER!

WELL DONE TRACY!

MAGNIFICENT!

A TRUE STAR IS BORN!

sweeties

yum!

**5.** My all-time favourite sweets are Smarties. Hint, hint, hint!

○ FACT OR ○ FIB

**6.** Mrs Darlow made me clean the classroom as punishment for bouncing my fist up and down on Justine Serves-Her-Right Littlewood's nose.

○ FACT OR ○ FIB

**7.** The Quiet Room is where naughty children go to reflect on their bad behaviour. Of course, I've never been sent there!

○ FACT OR ○ FIB

**8.** Cam's friend Jane is really big and bossy but she's pretty good at football. She's even better than Football at football!

○ FACT OR ○ FIB

This is getting silly!

**9.** On Christmas Day Cam let me peel lots of potatoes to make a huge plateful of crunchy golden chips topped with beans.

○ FACT OR ○ FIB

**10.** We have this pet rabbit at the Dumping Ground. It's a bit limp, like its name — Lettuce.

○ FACT OR ○ FIB

Now count up your scores!

# 1-3 CORRECT

Ha-ha! I really pulled the wool over your eyes, didn't I? You'll have to read all four of my Heartbreakingly Tragic real-life stories to brush up on your Beaker knowledge!

# 4-6 CORRECT

So I may have told a few tiny white lies in my time. But I'm usually Totally Truthful — honest! I mean, who else would tell Elaine that her bum looked especially big in her new white trousers?

# 7-10 CORRECT

Okay, okay, you got me! I promise I'll tell the truth from now on and I'll behave so beautifully even narky Miss Brown will give me a Gold Star! Speaking of stars, did I ever tell you my mum is this Ultra Glamorous Hollywood actress...?

ANSWERS: 1. FIB — Tracy borrows Adele's makeup. 2. FIB — Mike rescues Tracy from the top of a tree! 3. FIB — Tracy plays the part of Ebenezer Scrooge. 5. FACT. 6. FIB — Tracy had to clean the entire hall floor, not the classroom. 7. FIB — Tracy has spent many hours in the Quiet Room! 8. FACT. 9. FIB — Tracy's chips were topped with a runny egg. 10. FACT.

# Tracy + You = BFF?

Could you be my new BF?

## START
My bedroom is...

**MESSY** → Truth or dare?

**NEAT & TIDY** → I like to read...

**DARE** → I get top marks for...

**TRUTH** → At a sleepover I'd share my...

**BOOKS** → Truth or dare?

**MAGAZINES** → Your secrets are safe with me.

**GOOD BEHAVIOUR** → At a sleepover I'd share my...

**MY STORIES** → My friends say I'm...

**CARING** → At a sleepover I'd share my...

**FUNNY** → I'd never ever...

**EMBARRASSING MOMENTS** → Your secrets are safe with me.

**SPOOKIEST STORY** → I'd never ever...

**READ SOMEONE'S DIARY** → Your secrets are safe with me.

**NOT A CHANCE!** → NO.1 ENEMIES!

**FOREVER & EVER** → GREAT MATES!

**CRY** → SISTER WRITERS!

## NO.1 ENEMIES!
Friends Forever? More like Forever Foes! You're totally outgoing and confident — in fact, you're just too much like Tracy to ever get along. However, you would make a super challenger in the Dare Game. Tracy Beaker better watch out!

74

## GREAT MATES!
Like Peter, you're sensitive and caring — the best kind of friend! You'd always be there for Tracy, even if she called you names or lost her temper. Maybe your sweet nature would even rub off on Tracy and she'd become a kind, gentle little girl...? Perhaps not.

## SISTER WRITERS!
You're both full of imagination, bursting with incredible story ideas and wild daydreams, and destined to be super story writers, naturally. What a dynamic duo! Actually, the thought of *two* Tracy Beakers is a little bit terrifying...

Fast car

vroom!

Tracy's Super-Luxury Life!

Dream house

# Beaker's Bedrooms

## Enter at your peril...

### Cam's house

Call this a bedroom? I specifically requested a king-size bed, draped in white satin sheets with piles of fluffy cushions and a dressing table fit for a film star. Instead I got this

Watch out for my army of Killer Vampire bats! Hey, why don't bats live alone? Because they like to hang out with their friends! Ha!

Is it any wonder I look so Utterly Miserable and Broken-Hearted?

Okay, so Cam *did* let me paint everything black and she even stuck lots of luminous stars on the ceiling. They go twinkle twinkle twinkle all night long – not that the Brave and Brilliant Tracy Beaker is scared of the dark!

Just try to get past my Highly Poisonous, man-eating python. He has a particular liking for highly irritating, friend-stealing, green-jumper wearing individuals. (This means you Justine Littlewood!)

THIS ROOM BELONGS TO
TRACY BEAKER
**STRICTLY PRIVATE**
KEEP OUT ON PAIN OF DEATH.
AND IT WILL BE A <u>VERY</u> PAINFUL
DEATH TOO.

Can't you **read**? Look, I'm not even going to bore you with the details. Let's just say that it's practically a prison cell, with barely enough room to swing a cat. Honestly, I'm supposed to be in care — I should at least have a flat–screen TV, a four poster bed and a laptop to distract me from my Overwhelming Grief and Abandonment Issues.

We've each got our own rooms but don't think for one moment I've got any privacy. A certain Sneaky Someone snuck into my room only this morning and crayoned on my most Cherished Possession.

**CONFIDENTIAL**

# My Secret House!

I came across this empty house one day and decided to make it my own. That was until Alexander came along. Still, we fixed it up with cushions and throws and now it looks proper homely. Dead classy, isn't it?

Sometimes Football hangs out with us and we play the Dare Game. I always win, naturally!

This is the stereo

This is the mirror

This is the cupboard

This is the television

My new mate, Alexander. He's a bit of a drip, really, but he always brings along tasty snacks for us to snaffle. Yum, yum!

77

# Beakerise This Bedroom!

Create the perfect bedroom for The Amazing Tracy Beaker!

What will it be like? Here are some suggestions

## BED
Will Tracy have special bunk beds so she can always sleep in the top one — or will she have a king-size bed with heart-shaped cushions? What colour will her bed covers be and will she make her bed every morning, or leave it messy?

## WINDOW
Tracy spends a lot of time looking out of the window, so will she like lots of fluffy cushions on a window seat to make it more comfortable for her? Will she like glamorous sparkly curtains with gold stars on them, or a big black blind so she can have some privacy?

## ON THE WALLS
What will Tracy have stuck on the walls? Will she have a big photograph of her mum in a big fancy gold frame, or maybe some of her own drawings? Or will she have a pinboard with lots of different stuff stuck on it?

## ACCESSORIES
Will Tracy have nice ornaments and vases of flowers dotted around her room — or will it be really messy and scattered with midnight feast crumbs and socks? You could also give Tracy her own telephone so she can call Cam whenever she likes!

## FURNITURE
Will Tracy have a glamorous wardrobe where she can keep lots of posh party frocks, and will there be a desk with a notepad and pen where she can write lots of stories? Will she have a couch to relax on, or maybe just a giant beanbag?

# Tracy Goes To HOLLYWOOD

vroom!

Tracy has an invite to the poshest party around...
but what on earth will she wear?

Tracy always dreams about Hollywood as that's where her mum lives, making movies and being a very glamorous actress. But what if Tracy found herself in Hollywood one day, with her mum and an invitation to one of the poshest parties around? She could walk up the red carpet with the crowd shouting her name and asking for her autograph, but what should she wear? You decide!

**HAIR** Tracy isn't the biggest fan of her hair, so if she was going to a glamorous party then she might have it blow-dried straight. You could draw her hair all shiny and glossy and cascading down her back — or maybe she would have it in a fancy up-do?

**DRESS** Create a posh party frock for Tracy! Will it have big puffed out sleeves and a frilly petticoat underneath, would it be covered in sparkly sequins? Maybe she'll have a big ribbon around her waist? It can be any colour you want!

**BAG** Every party outfit needs a glamorous bag to match! Will you give Tracy a tiny clutch bag that's covered in sparkling diamantes? Or will it have a beaded strap, or funky tassles, or be shaped like a McDonald's cheeseburger? Use your imagination!

**GLITZ AND SPARKLE**

You'll need some jewellery to complement Tracy's new outfit. She might like a posh pearl necklace and matching bracelet, or a diamond choker, or maybe she'd have some big dangly earrings? Here are some more ideas to get you thinking...

★ **Charm bracelet**
★ **A pretty brooch**
★ **Pendant necklace**
★ **A tiara fit for a princess!**
★ **Chunky rings (like Jacky's!)**

# Draw Tracy's new look here!

# Starz! TOTALLY TRACY!

**Starz!**

Celebs, Celebs, Celebs

Super-Star Birthday Competition

Don't miss this amazing interview with the world's most successful author, Tracy Beaker!

The Dumping Ground

**Starz! scoops an exclusive interview with Tracy Beaker! Our top celebrity writer has jotted down some questions for Tracy, but has left the answers up to you! Imagine *you're* Tracy and fill in the answers Beaker-style!**

Were you surprised by the success of your record–breaking, best–selling autobiography?

-----------------------------------

-----------------------------------

-----------------------------------

-----------------------------------

Life in the Dumping Ground didn't sound that pleasant. What advice would you give anyone who had to live in a children's home?

-----------------------------------

-----------------------------------

-----------------------------------

-----------------------------------

-----------------------------------

Who has been your biggest
inspiration?

----------------------------------------
----------------------------------------
----------------------------------------
----------------------------------------

Is there anyone who you would like
to thank for helping you with your
book?

----------------------------------------
----------------------------------------
----------------------------------------
----------------------------------------

What's the best thing about being a
mega-rich celebrity?

----------------------------------------
----------------------------------------
----------------------------------------
----------------------------------------

Everyone knows you were
magnificent in your school's
performance of *A Christmas
Carol*. Would you ever consider
an acting career?

----------------------------------------
----------------------------------------
----------------------------------------
----------------------------------------

HURRAY!

WELL DONE TRACY!

THE GREATEST PERFORMANCE EVER!

MAGNIFICENT!

A TRUE STAR IS BORN!

Who would you like to play you in
a movie about your life?

----------------------------------------
----------------------------------------
----------------------------------------
----------------------------------------

Now that you're
super-famous what's
next for Tracy Beaker?

----------------------------------------
----------------------------------------
----------------------------------------
----------------------------------------
----------------------------------------

# The Brilliant Beaker Awards!

## The Best Foster Mum Ever!

Winner: Cam

Tracy says —

"I first met Cam when I lived at the Dumping Ground, and we hit it off after Cam found out that I was a great author, too. She took me to McDonald's for Big Macs and gave me a Mickey Mouse pen — that's when I knew she would be my future foster mum. It was just a matter of time, really."

yum!

## Worst Friend In The World

Winner: Louise

Justine →

Tracy says —

"I have no idea how anyone could pick being friends with Justine-Snatch-My-Friend-Littlewood over the amazing Tracy Beaker, but that's exactly what happened! I just hope Louise realises what a terrible mistake she's made..."

## Most Glamorous Hollywood Actress Ever!

Winner: My Mum, Carly!

Tracy says — "My mum is so beautiful and pretty that she simply has to win the *Most Glamorous Hollywood Actress Ever* award! My mum is such a great actress, I think we might star in a blockbuster movie together some day — probably a movie about my amazing life so far!"

## The Most OK Friend Who Is A Boy (I Suppose...) Award!

Winner: Peter!

Tracy says —
"Even though he ruins my birthday every year by being born on the same day, and despite the fact that he is a snivelling, drivelling little wimp AND a boy, I guess Peter is OK. My problem is that I'm too kind-hearted not to give him an award. I'm just way too nice!"

## Most Annoying Social Worker!

Winner: Elaine the Pain

Tracy says —
"Elaine is my social worker and she is a right pain. That's why she has that hilarious nickname. I suppose she does try to help, but I don't know if that's a reasonable enough excuse for being that annoying!"

## The Most Brilliant Person Ever!

Winner: Tracy Beaker (Obviously)!

Tracy says — " Well, I am the greatest and most successful author of all time. If anything I should have won more awards, but I guess this one will have to do for now. Hooray for Tracy Beaker!"

Turn over for more award fun!

# Create Your Own Awards!

Which people in your life would you like to see win an award? What awards would they win? Complete this page by inventing your own award categories and explain who won and why!

Award: ....................................

Winner: ....................................

Comments: ....................................

....................................

....................................

....................................

....................................

Stick a photo of the winner here!

Award: ....................................

Winner: ....................................

Comments: ....................................

....................................

....................................

....................................

Stick a photo of the winner here!

Award: ....................................

Winner: ....................................

Comments: ....................................

....................................

....................................

....................................

Stick a photo of the winner here!

Award: ....................................

Winner: ....................................

Comments: ....................................

....................................

....................................

....................................

Stick a photo of the winner here!

TRACY BEAKER AWARD

# Dani Harmer
## Talks Tracy Beaker!

⭐ **Do you miss playing Tracy?**

Yes, I miss her already! She's been a massive part of my life as I've played her for ten years. I'll miss her because she's been a brilliant character and I get to shout at people when I'm playing her, which is always fun!

⭐ **What's the best thing about Tracy?**

She looks out for the kids. She knows what it's like to be in care so everything she does is to make their lives better and I think that's really cute!

⭐ **What's the worst thing about her?**

Definitely her temper! She's got such a temper — more so when she was younger but even now if you cross her she will definitely have a go at you!

⭐ **Who's your favourite character, apart from Tracy, obviously?!**

I think my favourite character is Gus. He's the one I'd like to play if I was a little boy! He's an interesting character and also quite funny.

⭐ **Are you similar to Tracy?**

I can be quite stubborn but, other than that, I think we're complete opposites! I'm a lot more laid back but I suppose I can be a little bossy as well, just like Tracy...

89

**What's your top Jacqueline Wilson book?**
When I was growing up I read a lot of her books and it's really hard for me to pick one but I think probably *The Suitcase Kid* is my favourite. It helped me when my parents split up. Oh, and I love *Double Act* as well!

**What do you think of the outfits Tracy has worn throughout the series?**
Oh gosh, she's just one big fashion disaster! When she was younger her clothes were horrific and I used to absolutely dread putting them on but it did help me to get into character...

**Did you have any input into what she wore?**
I did when she was older and obviously she dressed a lot smarter as she's at work but when she was younger, No, otherwise I wouldn't have worn half of what she did!

**Can you tell us a secret about Dani Harmer?**
I have a fear of fish! I've had it since I was younger. I've no idea why but I just can't look at them — they're horrible!

**What was your top 'Tracy' moment throughout the whole series?**
Probably when Tracy got adopted by Cam. Cam did mess her around a bit – one minute she was fostered, then she was back at The Dumping Ground, then back living with Cam — so it was good for her character to just finally have some closure. When Cam adopted her she started to calm down a bit so I think that was my top moment!

Cam

**Now tell us a secret about Tracy...**
She's not as tough as she makes out. Obviously you wouldn't want to cross her but it's unlikely that she would do anything rather than shout her mouth off. She's a big softy really!

⭐ Tell us a behind the scenes secret from the Tracy Beaker set!

We filmed in an old school and the rooms in the Dumping Ground you see on TV used to be part of the school. There are quite a lot of fake walls — you can't tell when you watch but a lot of the walls move to let the cameras and cables go through!

⭐ Did everyone hang out together behind the scenes when you were filming?

Yes, we all stayed in the same apartment block. We were literally with each other 24/7 and it was so much fun!

⭐ How long does it take to learn your lines?

I've got a brilliant short term memory so it takes about ten minutes!

⭐ Who was the biggest prankster on set? Was there someone who played lots of jokes on the others?

Mia, Amy and Jessie who played Carmen, Tia and Lily. When those three got together a lot of mischief went on!

Who was your best friend in the Tracy Beaker cast?

Darragh, who plays Crash, was my best friend when we worked together and he's still my best friend now. He was in my series Dani's House with me as well. We've kind of grown up together and I speak to him every day.

dream house

Turn over for more!

91

# Dani's This Or That CHALLENGE!

Pizza OR Cakes?

Sunshine OR snow?

McDonald's OR KFC?

burger

yum!

Casual OR dressed up?

Curly OR straight hair?

Football OR tennis?

Seaside OR city?

# Tracy Beaker – What Happens Next?

Boo–hoo! The last ever episode of *Tracy Beaker Returns* saw Tracy leave the Dumping Ground!

The Dumping Ground

Now what will happen to her and the people who became her family there? Here are some ideas to get you thinking —

★ How will Tracy's new job work out? She might lose her temper with her new boss...

★ Will she see her Dumping Ground friends again? Could any of them become a best friend to her away from the home?

★ Now that she's older, what are Tracy's thoughts about her real mum?

★ Does she ever still wish it was her and Carly together, instead of Cam?

★ Will Tracy foster some Dumping Ground kids herself or adopt one as her own?

★ Could she ever become as super–annoying as social worker, Elaine the Pain?

It's up to you to write the next episode in Tracy's life so get busy!

# IMAGINE IF...
## ... you were Tracy Beaker!

It's all about the glamour dahlings!

⭐ Jacqueline Wilson and Nick Sharratt would be your besties.

Photography by Trish Beswick

⭐ Your mum would be a marvellous movie star.

⭐ You would be an Unbelievably Talented Writer and future Author Extraordinaire!

⭐ You would absolutely be The Most Fabulous and Famous Girl in the World!

Mmmm — worms! Yum yum!

⭐ You would have appeared on TV, in four books about you and in amazing exhibitions.

⭐ You would be the Undefeated Champion of Dares.

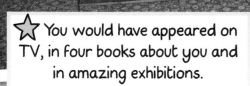

⭐ You would have exacted the Ultimate Revenge by gunking Justine Soooo–Lame Littlewood!

93

# DON'T MISS!

Click on

## www.jw-mag.com

for more info!

You can see even more of ME...

...and all your fave JW characters....